THE WORLD'S OF BLU

HALEY BRANTON
ANTHONY BRANTON

My daughter Haley inspired me to write this book during her battle with Leukemia. Watching her be brave and build up courage to fight this life threatening battle and knowing there was nothing I could do to help her. I felt helpless... So Haley and I thought maybe we could help other children learn to build their courage and strength to help them fight their battle and so thats what we did. Haley came up with the theme and gave me the ideas and I put them into a story. I am happy to say that Haley is currently cancer free and living her life to the fullest. I want to thank everyone for their love and support during her journey.

On a planet far far away there lived a little boy named Blu, which fit his personality because that is exactly how he felt every day. You see Blu did not like new things, in fact he was afraid of anything he did not understand and moving to this new town did not make it any easier. Blu did not like feeling this way. He thought to himself if only I had my own world that I could make my own friends and no one would laugh at me, everyone would love me.

That very night before he got ready for bed he walked over to his dad wrapped in the blanket he would usually use for hiding in and asked, "How do you meet new people that you never met before?" Blu's dad looked at him and smiled as he said, "Son, I wasn't always outgoing. A little girl from far far away helped me on my journey of not being afraid to find my courage." Blu interrupted, "can we go see her dad please? Or better yet can you talk to her for me and then she will give you some courage for me and I won't be afraid like you." Blu's dad said, "This is one trip you have to make alone, besides there's only room for one." Blu did not understand. "I'm only 6 dad, I can't do that! I'm scared!" said Blu. "There's nothing to be afraid of, it's in the safest place in the world and only you have the powers to get there. It's the same way I did...IMAGINATION!"

"What is imagination?" asked Blu. Blu's dad explained, "It's the ability to form new images and sensations in your mind that cannot be see or touched by others, and combined with your dreams you'll go far." Blu's dad pointed up at the night sky, there were billions of stars. The biggest planet he could see was red, the other one was blue and that was the one that Blu was most interested in because it was the furthest away and of course it was Blue. Blu could not wait to use his new powers called imagination! But first he thought to himself, "I must plan for this."

Blu ran to the kitchen grabbed his lunch box and filled it with two of every snack he could think of. Then he raced up stairs to grab his suitcase and he also filled it with everything he could think of.

Next stop the bathroom, he had to brush his teeth because that was the rules before bed and Blu was ok with that because he doesn't like cavities, they gave him the creeps. Then Blu packed up his tooth brush. Mom and Dad came up stairs to tuck Blu in with a kiss. All packed up, Blue was ready he had his pajamas, boots and his blanket that he no longer used to cover his face, but instead it was his cape with his best friend teddy by his side. Blu was ready, but first he had to activate his powers.

Blu sat on his bed and raised his hand up towards the night sky then laid down as he stared out his window at the beautiful stars. Blu's eyes started to close and then he started to float.....

Blu opened his eyes and he could not believe what he saw and he wasn't even afraid. He saw himself sleeping. As he soared higher and higher with his best friend Teddy by his side, Blu was on his way to get his courage. As Blue got closer to the stars, the red planet was getting bigger and bigger. This was the most amazing site he had ever seen. Blu flew towards the now big red planet, he did not see anyone.

The only signs of life Blu could see was a big sized radio controlled car with 3 wheels on each side and the words N.A.S.A on it with a picture of the blue Planet on it. Then Blu realized he was not that far away. Most of all he was excited to meet the little girl so he could receive his courage. As Blu got closer to the blue planet he realized something, he did not know anyone or anything about this beautiful place. What if people (kids) laugh at him like the ones on his home planet? So that's when he decided to use his powers of IMAGINATION to give himself the ability to be invisible to anyone or anything that made him nervous.

Right then Blu felt himself waking up so he rushed back to his home planet. That morning Blu told his dad about everything he had seen and how he was so close to the blue planet and that he could not wait to go back. Every morning after that he woke up and he was so excited to go back and explore some more...and that was very unusual for Blu.

Once Blu arrived on earth he activated his powers of invisibility. Then Blu remembered there's only two places on his planet he felt the safest. The first was his home and the second was the hospital. Blu just knew the blue planet had to have one and he had to be there. The first hospital Blu saw was Marybridge Children's Hospital and in room #601, there he saw his first human girl. She could not see him or Teddy because they were invisible. Blu wanted to observe her, she had beautiful long hair and big beautiful brown eyes. Blu wanted so bad to talk to her, but he was afraid. Blu noticed she had tubes in her arm and she looked very fatigued (tired). The next few weeks Blu noticed she lost all of her hair, Blu was sad for her. At the same time Blu was speechless for she was not sad, she was happy. Blu had never met someone as brave with so much courage and energy, it was like she was never sick and she was happy.

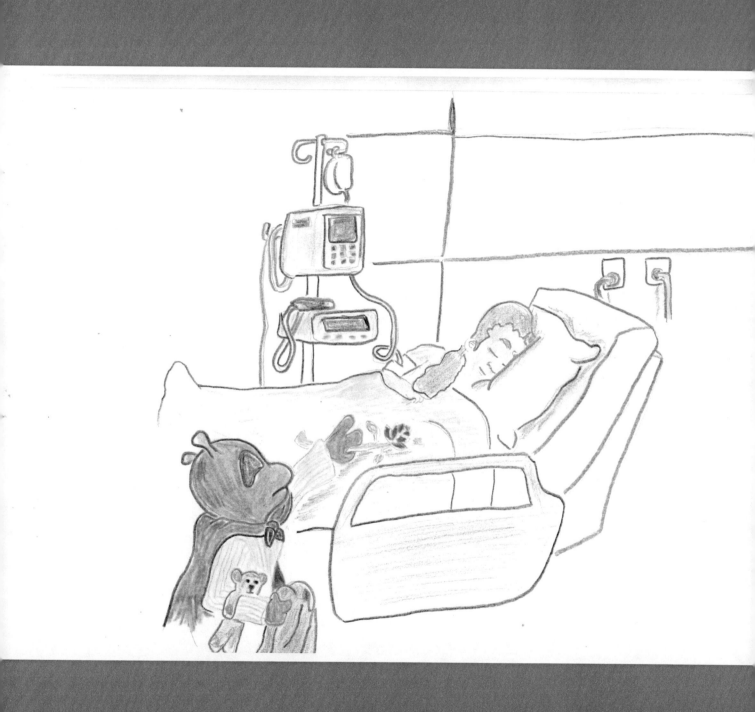

Months had passed by and one day Blu heard the news when the doctors told her mom and dad that she was no longer sick and that she can go home. Blue was so happy he turned off his power of invisibility to congratulate her. Right then he realized they had never met so he switched it back on....but not before she saw him, Blu stayed quiet. The little girl said "I saw you, you know." Blu said nothing. "If you're not going to say anything then how are we ever going to be friends? My name is Haley, what's yours?" Blu responded... "My name is Blu, but I don't want you to laugh at me because I look different." Haley responded, "My mom and dad told me that is what makes us unique, special one of a kind and that is what makes us valuable to the planet we live on and the people around us. My dad and mom say I give them hope, inspiration and strength. That's what keeps them looking forward to the next day. Without me, life would be hard to do...so I don't just fight for myself to get better, I fight for everyone even you Blu. I will never laugh at you, only with you because that's what friends do. We are friends right?" Blu revealed himself with teddy by his side, "Yes we are!" It was not long before Blu and Haley were talking all night. Haley told Blu, "When I first got to the hospital I was scared because I had never been to the hospital before. The nurse gave me medicine to help me relax and I fell asleep. When I awoke there where tubes in my arms and that made me nervous. My doctor explained that it was the best way for me to get my medicine, even when I slept. The doctor called it a PICC Line. It was better than needles getting poked in my arm all the time. I don't like getting needle pokes." Haley also talked about other fun stuff in the hospital like when she met the Nail Fairy and all her new friends who were sick like her. Blu talked about how it's so hard to make friends and how he so desperately needed courage to try new things.

Haley looked at Blu and said "You are Courage, you travelled through space to meet someone you never met before and if that's not courage I don't know what is. Also you can't get something you already have and when I unlocked my courage cancer never had a fighting chance." Haley also told Blu about how excited she is to go back to school and see her friends. Blu said, "But you look different, now the other kids will laugh at you like they do to me. What will you do?" Haley replied, "I will just tell them this is what you look like after defeating a notorious killer called Cancer. When they hear that, they will beg me to protect them." "Wow, how did you unlock your courage?" blu said. "My mom", replied Haley. Haley then told Blu the story that her mom told her when she was a little girl and how she helped another little boy from a far way planet. "That was my dad!" Blu said excitedly. Haley said, "When you go home you should try introducing yourself to new kids, look how well it worked for us." Blu felt really good about himself. Haley became Blu's best friend. Blu taught Haley how to mix her imagination with her sleep and Haley taught Blue how to unlock his courage.

Together they explored Worlds to help unlock the courage in every little girl and boy throughout the galaxy.

These pictures were the inspiration for the book "The Worlds of Blu", they were made by Haley who had leukemia.

Thank you for everyone who supported Haley and her family threw out her journey and long after!

Made in the USA
San Bernardino, CA
15 November 2017